WHERE DO THE BUGS GO WHEN it RAINS?

WRitten and IllUSTRATED BY
LAURAL FARABAUGH

First published in Maryland, USA, 2018
ISBN-13: 978-1983946097   ISBN-10: 1983946095

Dedicated to my loving family,
Keith, Jenna and Molly

My name is Little Miss Honey Bee.
It's a rainy day and I want you to come with me.
We will go together to fly about,
while I show you where the bugs hang out.

When it rains, the ladybug showers
under the water drops of yellow sunflowers.

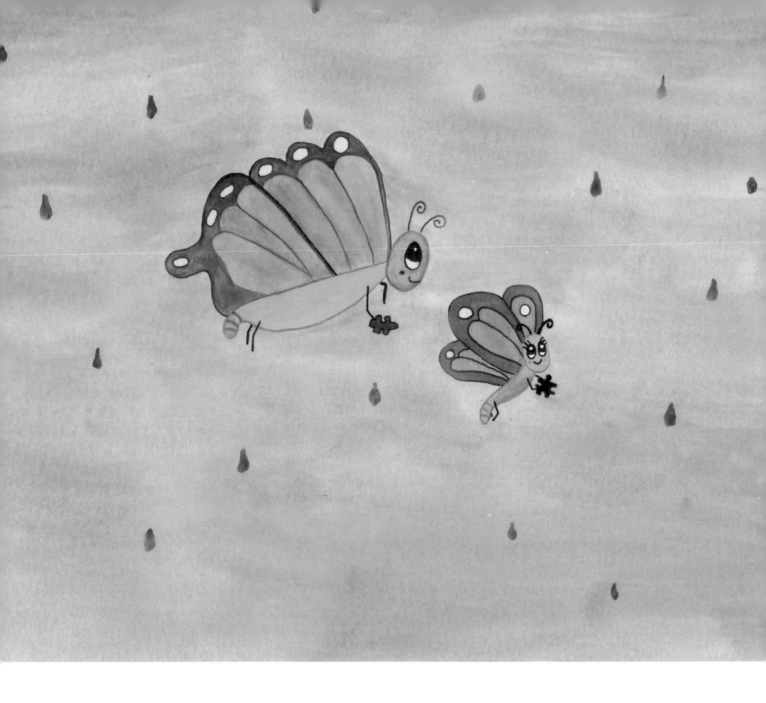

When it rains, butterflies like to put puzzles together,

to show their friends what they do in the yucky weather.

When it rains, the caterpillar puts on his favorite boots,
to jump in the puddles, splash and have a hoot.

When it rains, puddles are made in the grass.
Dragonflies like to pull their friends very fast.

When it rains, grasshoppers go to the puddles in a dash,

so excited to jump and make a big splash.

When it rains, the spiders mop their web up so high,

to keep them happy, safe and dry.

When it rains, the red ants have a fun snack to eat,
but some take time for a long, long sleep.

When it rains, praying mantises aren't afraid of gray skies.
They get busy making yummy mud pies.

When it rains, mushrooms keep bugs dry all day,

so they have fun reading until it's time to play.

Whenit rains, the bugs go to the ground below,
to watch an exciting picture show.

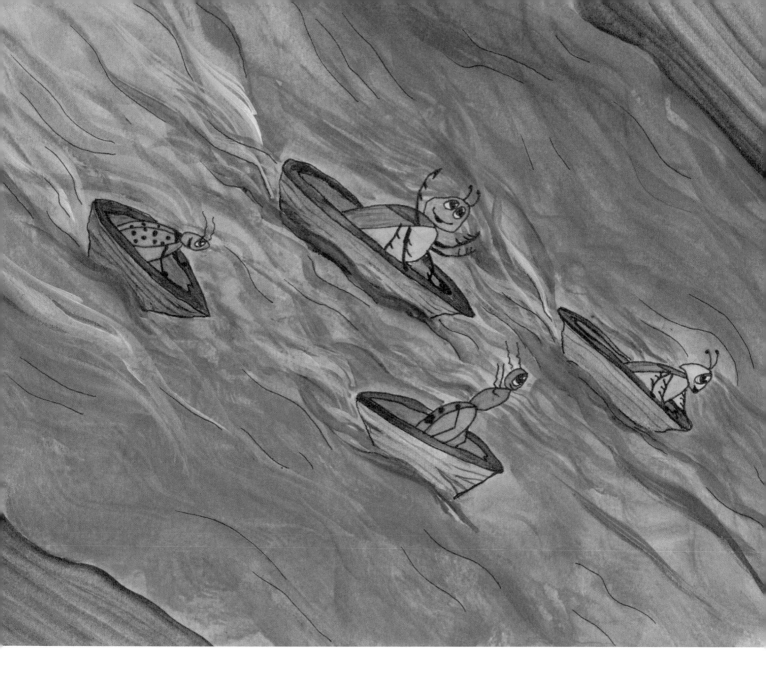

When it rains, bugs dash to tell,
who has chosen the fastest nut shell.

When it rains music is made by water drops,

ants love to dance to until it stops.

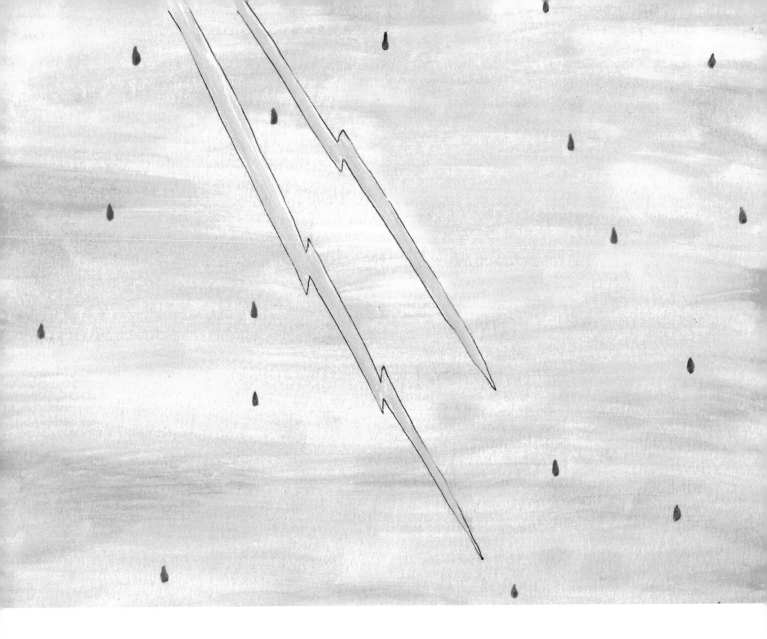

When it rains, lightning scares the baby bugs,

so Mama cuddles them with her hugs.

Little Miss Honey Bee wonders,
"What will the bugs want to do now?",

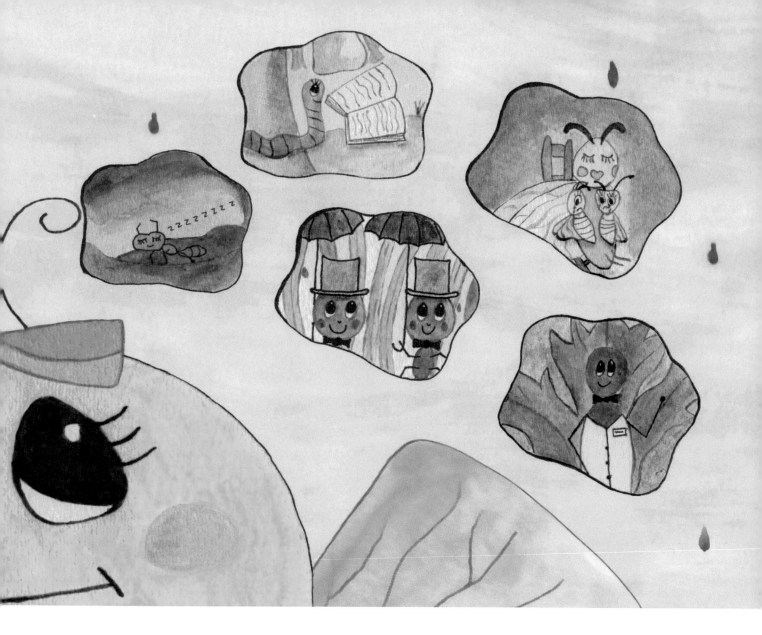

as the rain begins to slow down.

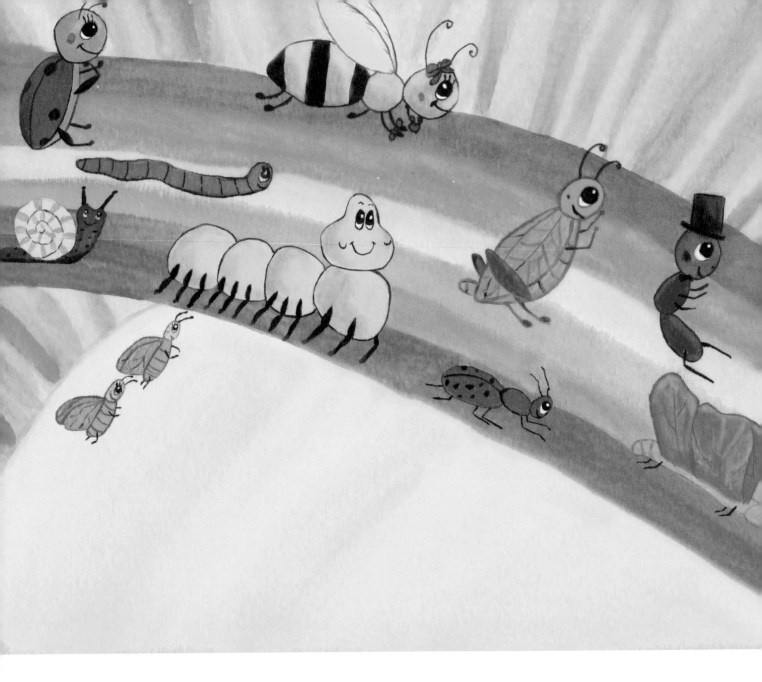

A rainbow appears with the sunshine at last.
All the bug friends end their day with a blast.

When it rains, the showers keep the bugs so busy.
See, having fun in the rain is easy.

The End

Also Available:

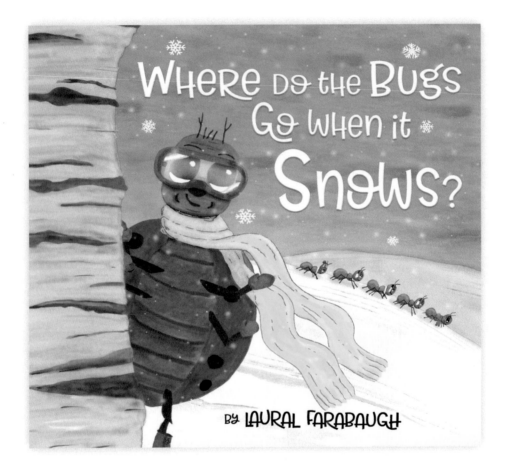

Visit www.LauralFarabaughBooks.com

Made in the USA
Monee, IL
02 February 2020